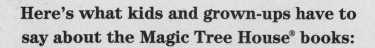

**Here's what kids and grown-ups have to
say about the Magic Tree House® books:**

"Oh, man . . . the Magic Tree House series
is really exciting!"
—Christina

"I like the Magic Tree House series. I stay up
all night reading them. Even on school nights!"
—Peter

"Jack and Annie have opened a door to a world
of literacy that I know will continue throughout
the lives of my students."
—Deborah H.

"As a librarian, I have seen many happy young
readers coming into the library to check out
the next Magic Tree House book in the series."
—Lynne H.

MAGIC TREE HOUSE® #32
A MERLIN MISSION

Winter of the Ice Wizard

by Mary Pope Osborne

illustrated by Sal Murdocca

A STEPPING STONE BOOK™

Random House 🏠 New York

For Sal Murdocca,
Wizard of Wondrous Art

Text copyright © 2004 by Mary Pope Osborne
Cover art and interior illustrations copyright © 2004 by Sal Murdocca

All rights reserved. Published in the United States by Random House Children's Books, a division of Penguin Random House LLC, New York. Originally published in hardcover in the United States by Random House Children's Books, New York, in 2004.

Random House and the colophon are registered trademarks and A Stepping Stone Book and the colophon are trademarks of Penguin Random House LLC. Magic Tree House is a registered trademark of Mary Pope Osborne; used under license.

Visit us on the Web!
SteppingStonesBooks.com
randomhousekids.com
MagicTreeHouse.com

Educators and librarians, for a variety of teaching tools, visit us at
RHTeachersLibrarians.com

The Library of Congress has cataloged the hardcover edition of this work as follows:
Osborne, Mary Pope.
Winter of the ice wizard / by Mary Pope Osborne ; illustrated by Sal Murdocca. — 1st ed.
p. cm. — (Magic tree house ; #32)
Summary: Jack and Annie are joined by Teddy and Kathleen as they travel to the snowy Land-Behind-the-Clouds, where they search for the eye of the Ice Wizard and attempt to help Merlin and Morgan.
"A Stepping Stone book."
ISBN 978-0-375-82736-5 (trade) — ISBN 978-0-375-92736-2 (lib. bdg.) —
ISBN 978-0-375-89454-1 (ebook)
[1. Space and time—Fiction. 2. Magic—Fiction. 3. Wizards—Fiction.]
I. Murdocca, Sal, ill. II. Title. III. Series: Osborne, Mary Pope.
Magic tree house series ; v #32.
PZ7.O81167Wi 2004 [Fic]—dc22 2004002802

ISBN 978-0-375-87395-9 (pbk.)

Printed in the United States of America

22 21 20 19 18 17 16 15 14 13

This book has been officially leveled by using the F&P Text Level Gradient™ Leveling System.

CONTENTS

Dear Reader,

Winter of the Ice Wizard *is the fourth "Merlin Mission" in the Magic Tree House series. In these books, Merlin the magician sends Jack and Annie on their tree house adventures to mythical lands.*

In the first Merlin Mission, Christmas in Camelot, *Jack and Annie journey to the Otherworld to find a magical cauldron that holds the Water of Memory and Imagination. Then in* Haunted Castle on Hallows Eve, *they rescue the stolen Diamond of Destiny with the help of their* *friend Teddy. In <u>Summer of the Sea Serpent</u>, Jack and Annie travel to an enchanted seacoast, where they find the hidden Sword of Light with Teddy and a seal girl named Kathleen.*

Now, on the first day of winter, Jack and Annie are about to head out on another magical mission. They invite you to join them. But be sure to wear warm clothes and snow boots. You're going to a very cold land where very weird things happen. . . .

Mary Pope Osborne

The fetters shall break
And the wolf run free.
Secret things I know
And onward see.
           —From *The Poetic Edda*

CHAPTER ONE

Winter Solstice

A cold wind rattled the windowpanes. But inside the house, it was warm and cozy. Jack and Annie were making Christmas cookies with their mom. Jack pressed a star-shaped cookie cutter into the dough.

"Hey, it's snowing outside," said Annie.

Jack looked out the window. Huge snowflakes were falling from the late-afternoon sky.

"You want to go out?" asked Annie.

"Not really. It'll be dark soon," said Jack.

"That's right," said their mom. "Today's the first day of winter. It's the shortest day of the year."

Jack's heart skipped a beat. "You mean it's the *winter solstice*?" he said.

"Yes," said their mom.

Annie gasped. "The winter solstice?" she said.

"Yes . . . ," their mom said, puzzled.

Jack and Annie looked at each other. Last summer, Merlin the magician had called for their help on the *summer* solstice. Maybe he would need them again today!

Jack put down the cookie cutter and wiped his hands on a towel. "Actually, Mom, it might be fun to play in the snow for just a few minutes," he said.

"Whatever you want," their mom said. "Just dress warmly. I'll finish up with the cookies and put them in the oven."

"Thanks!" said Jack. He and Annie raced to the closet and pulled on their boots. They threw on jackets, scarves, gloves, and caps.

"Be home before dark," their mom said.

"We will!" called Jack.

"Bye, Mom!" Annie shouted.

Jack and Annie slipped out of their house into the snowy cold. Their boots squeaked as they ran across their white yard and headed toward the Frog Creek woods.

At the edge of the woods, Jack stopped. He couldn't believe how beautiful the trees looked. White powder covered the branches of the hemlocks and pines.

"Look," said Annie. She pointed to two pairs of footprints that led out to the road and then back into the woods. "Somebody else has been here."

"It looks like they were walking out of the woods—but turned back," said Jack. "Let's hurry!" If the magic tree house *had* come back today, he didn't want anyone else finding it first!

Jack and Annie walked quickly through the woods, following the two sets of footprints.

"Stop!" said Annie. She pulled Jack behind a tree. "Over there!"

Through the falling snow, Jack saw two people in long, dark cloaks. They were hurrying toward a tall oak—and high in the oak was the magic tree house!

"Oh, no!" said Jack.

The tree house *was* back! And someone else had found it!

"Hey!" Jack yelled. "Stop!" The tree house had come for him and Annie—no one else!

Jack started running. Annie followed. Jack slipped and fell in the snow, but he scrambled up and kept going. By the time he and Annie got to the tree house, the two people had climbed up the rope ladder and disappeared inside.

"Come out!" Jack yelled.

"This is *our* tree house!" shouted Annie.

Two kids poked their heads out of the tree house window. They both looked like they were about thirteen years old. The boy had tousled red hair and freckles. The girl had sea-blue eyes and long, curly black hair. Their cheeks were rosy from the cold. They laughed when they saw Jack and Annie.

"Excellent!" said the boy. "We came to find you, but you have found us instead."

"Teddy!" cried Annie. "Kathleen! Hi!"

Teddy was the young sorcerer who worked with Morgan in her library in Camelot. Kathleen was the enchanted selkie girl who'd helped Jack and Annie on the summer solstice by magically turning them all into seals.

Jack was stunned. He had never imagined that their two friends from Camelot might someday visit Frog Creek! "What are you guys doing here?" he shouted.

"Climb up and we will tell you!" said Teddy.

Jack and Annie hurried up the rope ladder. When they climbed inside the tree house, Annie threw her arms around Teddy and Kathleen. "I can't believe you came to visit us!" she said.

"It pleases me to see you, Annie," said Kathleen. "And you also, Jack." Her large blue eyes sparkled.

"It pleases me, too," Jack said shyly. He still thought Kathleen was the most beautiful girl he had ever seen. Even when she'd been a seal, she'd been lovely.

"We went looking for you!" said Teddy. "We climbed down and walked through the woods to a road."

"But the road was full of monsters!" said Kathleen. "A big red creature nearly ran over us! It made a honking sound!"

"Then before we knew it, a giant black monster charged at us! It had a ferocious growl!" said Teddy. "We came back here to gather our wits."

"Those weren't monsters!" said Annie, laughing. "They were just cars!"

"Cars?" said Teddy.

"Yeah, they have motors and people drive them," said Jack.

"Motors?" said Teddy.

"It's hard to explain," said Annie. "Just remember—in our world, you have to watch out for cars every time you cross a road."

"Indeed we will," said Teddy.

"Why have you come here?" asked Jack.

"We found a message for you in Merlin's chambers," said Teddy, "and decided to deliver it ourselves."

"So we climbed into the tree house outside Morgan's library," said Kathleen. "Teddy pointed to the words *Frog Creek* in the message and made a wish to come here. The next thing we knew, we were here in these woods."

Teddy pulled a small gray stone from his cloak. "And *this* is the message we brought you," he said.

Jack took the stone from Teddy.

The message was written in tiny hand-writing. Jack read it aloud:

To Jack and Annie of Frog Creek:
My Staff of Strength has been stolen.
On the winter solstice, journey to the
Land-Behind-the-Clouds. Travel
toward the setting sun and retrieve my
staff—or all will be lost.
Merlin

"Oh, wow," said Annie. "That sounds serious."

"Yeah," said Jack. "But why didn't Merlin send us the message himself?"

"We do not know," said Teddy. "Neither Merlin nor Morgan has been seen for days."

"Where did they go?" asked Annie.

"'Tis a mystery," said Teddy. "Last week I journeyed to the selkie cove to bring Kathleen to Camelot. She is going to be a helper in Morgan's library. But when we returned, we could not find Merlin or Morgan."

"We only found this message for you," said Kathleen.

"Aye, and I thought that when Merlin *does* return," said Teddy, "he will be greatly pleased to have his staff back. Much of his power comes from its ancient and mysterious magic."

"Wow," said Annie.

"In his message, he tells us to go to the Land-Behind-the-Clouds," said Jack. "Where's that?"

"'Tis a land far north of my cove," said Kathleen. "I have never journeyed there."

"Nor I," said Teddy. "But I have read about it in Morgan's books. 'Tis as bleak as a frozen white desert. I am eager to see it for myself."

"So you and Kathleen are coming with us?" said Annie.

"Indeed!" said Kathleen.

"Great!" said Jack and Annie together.

"If we all work together, we can do anything, aye?" said Teddy.

"Aye!" said Annie.

I hope so, thought Jack.

Annie pointed at the words *Land-Behind-the-Clouds* in Merlin's message. "Okay, ready?" she said to the others.

"Yes!" said Kathleen.

"I guess so," said Jack.

"Onward!" said Teddy.

"I wish we could all go there!" Annie said.

The tree house started to spin.

It spun faster and faster.

Then everything was still.

Absolutely still.

CHAPTER TWO

Land-Behind-the-Clouds

Jack felt the sharp bite of an icy wind. He looked out the window with the others. "Oh, man," he whispered.

The tree house was not in a tree—for there were no trees anywhere to be seen. Instead, it was sitting high on top of a steep snowdrift. Other drifts rose and fell across a vast snowy plain. Beyond the plain were hills and mountains.

"The books were right," said Teddy, his teeth chattering. "'Tis bleak here indeed."

"No, 'tis lovely," said Kathleen. "'Tis the land where the northern seal people live."

"Cool," said Annie.

Jack dug his hands into his pockets. He agreed with Teddy. The land did seem bleak—and freezing! "I wonder where Merlin's Staff of Strength is," he said, shivering.

"Let us begin our search!" said Kathleen. "The message tells us we must travel toward the setting sun."

Kathleen climbed out of the tree house window. She gathered her cloak around her and sat down on top of the snowdrift. Then she pushed off and slid down the steep slope.

"Oh, wow. Wait for me!" called Annie. She climbed out the window and followed Kathleen. Whooping, she slid to the bottom of the snowdrift. "Come on, you guys! It's fun!" she shouted.

Jack and Teddy looked at each other. "Shall we?" said Teddy. Jack nodded. He pulled his scarf tighter around his neck and followed Teddy out of the window.

Jack and Teddy sat down side by side. They pushed off and slid down the icy snowdrift. Jack couldn't help whooping, too. It *was* fun.

At the bottom of the drift, Jack and Teddy scrambled to their feet. Jack brushed the snow off his clothes. He could see his breath in the frigid air.

"It's j-just a little chilly," said Annie, hugging herself.

Only Kathleen seemed not to mind the cold. She was smiling as she lay on the ground, gazing up at the sky. *Her seal nature probably keeps her warm,* Jack thought with envy.

Teddy peered across the snowy plain. "I believe not one living creature is here but us," he said.

"Not true at all," said Kathleen. She pointed upward. "I see snow geese and whistling swans."

"I can almost see them, too," said Annie.

Kathleen stood up. She shielded her eyes and gazed across the plain. The cold sun was low in the sky. It cast long blue shadows beneath the snowdrifts. She pointed into the distance. "And see? A white hare is leaping home before dark," she said.

Jack looked where Kathleen pointed, but he couldn't see anything moving at all.

"I see a snowy owl, too," said Kathleen, "and—oh, no!"

"What?" said Annie.

"Wolves," Kathleen said with a shudder. "They just disappeared behind a snowdrift. My people greatly fear the wolves."

"You need not be afraid. I shall protect you," said Teddy. He took Kathleen's hand. "Come! Let us make haste toward the sun!"

Together, Teddy and Kathleen headed across the snow-covered plain. Their woolen cloaks waved behind them. Annie and Jack dug their hands in their pockets and quickly followed them toward the setting sun.

As Teddy, Kathleen, Jack, and Annie trudged across the frozen plain, the sun sank closer and closer to the horizon. Its last rays poured purple-pink light over the snow.

The wind blew against Jack's face. He looked down and kept walking. The cold felt like needles on his skin. Each icy breath was painful. He hoped they found Merlin's Staff of Strength soon. He couldn't imagine anyone surviving for long in this lonely, freezing land.

Jack's thoughts were interrupted when he heard Annie calling. He looked up. The sun had completely slipped behind the horizon. In the cold twilight, the snow had faded from purple-pink to a dark shade of blue.

"Jack! Come look!" Annie called. She, Teddy, and Kathleen were standing on the slope of a huge snowdrift.

Jack hurried to join them.

"Look!" said Annie.

"Oh, man," Jack said softly.

On the other side of the snowdrift was a glimmering palace made from huge blocks of ice.

Beneath the rising moon, its gleaming spires pierced the blue dusk.

"I wonder who lives there . . . ," said Jack.

"Let us go and find out!" said Teddy.

Teddy led the way down the slope to the ice palace. Long icicles hung like spears in front of the entrance.

"It seems no one has visited this place in quite a while," said Kathleen.

"Indeed," said Teddy. He broke off several icicles, and they clattered to the ground. "Onward?" he said.

The others nodded.

Kicking aside the chunks of ice, Teddy led them all into the ice palace.

CHAPTER THREE

The Ice Wizard

The air inside the palace was even colder than the air outside. Moonlight flooded through tall arches in the walls. The floor shined like a skating rink. Thick columns of sparkling ice held up a domed ceiling.

"WELCOME, JACK AND ANNIE," boomed a voice from beyond the columns.

Jack gasped. "Is that Merlin?" he whispered.

"It does not sound like Merlin," whispered Teddy.

"But how does he know our names?" whispered Annie.

"COME, JACK AND ANNIE. I HAVE BEEN WAITING FOR YOU," bellowed the voice.

"Maybe it *is* Merlin!" said Annie. "Maybe he's just using a different voice! Come on!"

"Annie, wait!" Jack called. But Annie had already disappeared into the sparkly room. "We have to follow her," he said to Teddy and Kathleen.

The three of them hurried after Annie. Beyond the columns, steps made of carved ice led up to a platform. Sitting on a throne on the platform was a huge bearded man.

The man on the throne was definitely *not* Merlin. He was dressed in a worn robe trimmed with dirty fur. He had a rugged, weather-beaten face, a bushy beard, and a black eye patch. He leaned forward and glared down at Annie with his one good eye.

"Who are *you*?" he demanded. "I was expecting Jack and Annie of Frog Creek."

Annie stepped toward the throne. "I am Annie and he's Jack," she said. "And these are our friends Teddy and Kathleen. We come in peace."

"Annie? Jack?" the man snorted. "You are not Annie and Jack! You are far too small!"

"We're not so small," said Annie. "I'm nine. Jack's ten."

"But you are *children*," the man said with scorn. "Jack and Annie are heroes!"

"Well, I don't know if I'd call us heroes," said Annie. "But we sometimes help Merlin and Morgan le Fay."

"Annie, shhh!" said Jack. He didn't trust the man on the throne and worried that Annie was saying too much.

But Annie went on. "In fact, Merlin told us to come to the Land-Behind-the-Clouds today," she said. "He sent us a message written on a stone."

"Ah . . . ," said the man on the throne. "Perhaps you really are Jack and Annie." He leaned forward and spoke in a low voice:

To Jack and Annie of Frog Creek:

My Staff of Strength has been stolen. On the winter solstice, journey to the Land-Behind-the-Clouds. Travel toward the setting sun and retrieve my staff—or all will be lost.

Jack didn't understand. "How . . . ?"

"How do I know what was in Merlin's message?" the man said. "I know because I wrote it

myself! I hoped it would find its way to you somehow."

Jack stepped back. So Merlin hadn't sent them on this mission at all. The weird man on the throne had tricked them!

"Who are you?" demanded Teddy.

"I am the Ice Wizard," said the man. "The Wizard of Winter."

Teddy gulped.

Oh, no! thought Jack. They had heard about this wizard on their past Merlin missions. It was the Wizard of Winter who had put a spell on the Raven King and who had stolen the Sword of Light!

The wizard glanced coldly from Teddy to Kathleen. "And who are the two of you?"

"I am Teddy of Camelot," said Teddy. "I am an apprentice to Morgan le Fay, in training to be a sorcerer myself."

"A sorcerer?" said the wizard.

"Yes," said Teddy. "My father was a sorcerer. My mother was a wood sprite."

"And I am a selkie," said Kathleen, "one of the ancient seal people."

"So you are both from *my* world," said the Ice Wizard. "You are of no use to me." He looked back at Jack and Annie. "I am interested only in the two mortals, Jack and Annie of Frog Creek."

"Why are you interested in us?" said Jack.

"Because of what you have done for Merlin!" bellowed the Ice Wizard. "For Merlin, you found the Water of Memory and Imagination! For Merlin, you found the Diamond of Destiny! For Merlin, you found the Sword of Light! Now I want you to find something for *me*."

"What do you want us to find?" asked Annie.

The Ice Wizard grabbed the black patch covering his left eye. He yanked it off, revealing a dark, empty socket underneath.

"Yikes," Annie said softly.

"I want you to find my eye," the Ice Wizard said.

"Oh, man," said Jack. He was horrified.

"Are—are you quite serious?" said Teddy. "You want them to find your *eye*?"

The wizard covered his empty eye socket with the patch again. "Yes," he said. "I want Jack and Annie to find my eye—and bring it back to me."

"But—why?" said Jack. "Even if we found it, we couldn't make it work. We're not medical experts or anything."

"And anyway, why can't you get your eye yourself?" said Annie. "You're a wizard!"

"DO NOT QUESTION MY ORDERS!" the wizard roared at her.

"Hey, don't yell at my sister!" said Jack.

The wizard raised a bushy eyebrow. "You are brother and sister?" he said.

"Yes," said Jack.

The wizard nodded slowly. His voice grew softer. "And you protect your sister," he said.

"We protect each other," said Jack.

"I see," whispered the wizard. Then his voice turned gruff again. "Long ago, I traded my eye for something I wanted very much. But I never got what I wanted. So now I want my eye back."

"Who did you trade with?" asked Annie.

"The Fates!" said the wizard. "I traded with the Fates! But they cheated me! And that is why I sent for you and Jack. You must go to the Fates and find my eye, and you must go alone."

"Why alone?" asked Jack.

"Because only mortals can undo a bargain with the Fates," said the Ice Wizard, "not wizards like me—nor seal girls, nor the sons of sorcerers, like your two friends."

"But Jack and I succeeded in our other missions because Teddy and Kathleen or Morgan and Merlin helped us," said Annie.

"What kind of help did they give you?" said the wizard.

"Well, mostly magic rhymes and riddles," said Annie.

"Ah. Then I shall do the same," said the wizard. He thought for a moment, then leaned forward on his throne. In a growly voice, he said:

Take my sleigh
And find your way
To the House of the Norns
In the curve of the bay.

Pay them whatever
They tell you to pay.
And bring back my eye
By break of day.

The wizard reached into the folds of his ragged robe and pulled out a thick string with a row of knots. "This wind-string will speed you on your journey," he said. He tossed the string to Jack.

What's a wind-string? Jack wondered. *And who are the Norns?*

Before Jack could ask any questions, the Ice Wizard pointed at him. "Now listen carefully to this warning," he said. "Beware the white wolves of the night. They may follow you on your quest. Never let them catch up with you. If they catch you, they will eat you!"

Jack felt a chill run down his spine.

The Ice Wizard picked up a carved wooden stick from the floor beside his throne. Its smooth, polished wood glowed in the moonlight.

Teddy gasped. "'Tis Merlin's Staff of Strength!" he said.

"Indeed," said the wizard. He turned to Jack and Annie. "Go now and find my eye," he said. "Or you will never see Merlin and Morgan le Fay again."

"What have you done with them?" cried Annie.

The wizard stared at her coldly. "I will not tell you," he said. "You will see them again *only* if you return my eye before the break of day."

"But—" said Annie.

"No more questions!" said the wizard. "Be on your way!" Before any of them could speak, the Ice Wizard slashed the air with Merlin's Staff of Strength and shouted a spell—"OW-NIGH!"

A flash of blue fire shot from the end of the staff. In an instant, Jack, Annie, Teddy, and Kathleen found themselves outside the palace in the freezing night.

CHAPTER FOUR

Take My Sleigh

Jack sat on the frozen ground. Annie, Teddy, and Kathleen sat nearby. They were all too shocked to speak. The night was quiet. Overhead the full moon shined brightly, and a few cold stars twinkled in the clear sky.

Finally Annie broke the silence. "I wonder what he did to Merlin and Morgan," she said.

"I wonder where you will find his eye," said Teddy.

"I wonder how we'll carry it around," said Jack.

"And I wonder if the wolves are near," said Kathleen. She stood up and looked around, pulling her cloak tightly around her.

"Well, does anyone remember the Ice Wizard's rhyme?" said Teddy.

"Yes," said Kathleen. She repeated the rhyme perfectly by heart:

Take my sleigh
And find your way
To the House of the Norns
In the curve of the bay.
Pay them whatever
They tell you to pay
And bring back my eye
By break of day.

"What are *Norns*?" asked Jack.

"I have read about the Norns in Morgan's books," said Teddy. "They are known as the Sisters of Fate. They spend their days weaving great tapestries. Their weaving determines the fate of all who live in the Land-Behind-the-Clouds."

"So the Norns have his eye?" said Jack. "That's who he meant when he said he 'traded with the Fates'?"

"It would seem so," said Teddy.

"He said we should take his sleigh to find them," said Annie. "Where's his sleigh?"

"Look," said Kathleen, pointing. "'Tis there."

"Oh, wow," said Annie.

Not far away, a strange-looking silver sleigh glided silently from behind a snowbank. The sleigh looked like a small sailing ship with shiny runners. No one was steering it, and no horses or reindeer were pulling it. From its mast, a white sail drooped in the still air.

As the sleigh slid to a stop, an eerie howl shattered the calm of the windless night.

"Wolves!" cried Teddy. "Let us make haste!"

Kathleen grabbed his arm. "Do not run," she said. "If we run, they will chase us."

"Yes, of course," said Teddy. "They must not see that we are afraid."

Another howl shattered the air.

"Run!" cried Teddy.

They all charged across the snow to the sleigh and scrambled into it. Jack and Kathleen stood at the front, and Annie and Teddy stood at the back.

"There they are!" cried Teddy, pointing. "The white wolves of the night!"

Jack turned and saw two large white wolves dashing across the plain in the moonlight. As the wolves ran toward the sleigh, their big paws scattered snow around them.

"Go, go, go!" Jack cried, clutching the front of the sleigh.

But the sleigh didn't move. And the wolves kept coming. "How can we make it go?" cried Jack.

"Use the wind-string!" said Teddy.

Jack pulled the knotted string the wizard had given him out of his pocket. "Use it *how*?" he shouted.

"Untie a knot!" said Teddy.

Jack pulled off his gloves. His fingers were trembling as he tried to untie one of the knots. *This is crazy!* he thought. *How can untying a knot in a string help us?* But soon he managed to loosen one of the knots.

A cold breeze began blowing from behind the sleigh. It ruffled the sail overhead.

"Untie another!" shouted Teddy. "Hurry!"

Jack quickly untied a second knot. The breeze grew stronger, and the sail filled out a bit more. The sleigh's shiny runners began sliding across the snow.

"Yay!" called Annie. "It works!"

"Yes, but not nearly swiftly enough!" said Teddy.

Jack looked back. The two white wolves had almost caught up with them. They were yelping and running behind the sleigh. Their mouths were open, showing their sharp teeth.

Jack quickly untied a third knot. A cold wind blasted the sail. It opened with a snap, and the sleigh shot forward!

"Stand fast!" cried Teddy.

Jack, Annie, and Kathleen held tightly to the sides of the sleigh to keep from falling out. Teddy grabbed the rudder and steered them over the snow, away from the ice palace.

The wizard's sleigh zoomed across the frozen ground, leaving the white wolves in its wake. Their yelping noises grew fainter and fainter, until they could be heard no more.

The wind kept pushing the silver sleigh over the ice and snow. The runners made *swish-swish* sounds as they slid over the moonlit plain. The square sail billowed in the wind, like the sail of a Viking ship. With the wolves far behind, the ride was really fun, but cold.

"How did you know untying knots would make the wind blow?" Jack asked Teddy.

"'Tis an ancient magic," said Teddy. "I have read of wind-strings but had never seen one."

"It's a good thing you read so much," said Annie.

"Oh, look!" said Kathleen. "Hares and foxes!"

"Where?" said Annie.

"There!" Kathleen pointed into the dark distance. "Playing in the snow! And listen! Whistling swans—overhead, behind that cloud."

"Wow," said Annie.

Jack was amazed by Kathleen's power to see and hear so many things. As before, the moonlit landscape seemed completely empty to him.

"Where are you steering us?" Annie asked Teddy.

"I have no idea!" said Teddy, laughing.

"We're supposed to go to a curve of a bay to find the Norns," said Annie.

"Then turn left and follow the swans!" said Kathleen, pointing across the snowy plain. "They are flying toward the sea!"

Teddy swerved the sleigh to the left. For a while, they bounced up and down over the snow. Then the ride grew smoother.

"We are on sea ice now!" said Kathleen. "Seals are beneath! I see their breathing holes! Perhaps we should stop."

"Indeed!" said Teddy as they whizzed along. "But how?"

"Try *tying* a knot!" said Annie.

"Excellent idea!" said Teddy. "Jack?"

Jack yanked off his gloves. With cold, shaky fingers, he tied a knot in the string. The wind lessened a bit. The sleigh began to slow down.

He tied another. The sail started to droop.

"Hooray!" said Annie.

Jack tied a third knot and the wind completely died away. The sleigh glided to a stop.

"Well done!" said Teddy.

"Thanks," said Jack. He tucked the string back in his pocket and looked around. "I wonder if this is where the Norns live."

"I will ask," said Kathleen.

Ask who? thought Jack.

Kathleen climbed out of the sleigh. She walked over the sea ice, studying it closely. Then she stopped above a small hole.

Kathleen knelt down and spoke softly in selkie language. Then she put her ear close to the hole in the ice and listened.

A moment later, she stood up. "The seal told me the curve of the bay lies just beyond those sea rocks," she said, pointing. "That is where we will find the Norns."

"Great," said Annie.

Jack, Annie, Teddy, and Kathleen crunched over the frozen sea under the bright moon. They walked through a narrow passage between the sea rocks. When they stepped out from the passage, they stopped.

"There 'tis," said Teddy.

About fifty yards away was a large, snowy white mound. Smoke was coming from a chimney on top of the mound. Lantern light flickered from a small, round window.

"I know you must bargain for the Ice Wizard's eye alone," said Teddy. "But I would at least like to take a peek at the Norns."

He moved quietly to the window and peered into the house. The others joined him. They saw a large fire burning on a hearth. In its rosy glow, three strange creatures were weaving at a big loom. Jack caught his breath. Their appearance was shocking.

The three Sisters of Fate were as skinny as skeletons. They all had straggly hair, long noses, and huge, bulging eyes. Their crooked, bony fingers fluttered over a large tapestry.

Around the room other tapestries were stacked to the ceiling.

"They look like witches in a fairy tale," whispered Annie.

"Aye, but they are not witches," said Teddy. "Every cloth they weave is the history of a life."

"Wow," said Annie.

"Well, good luck," said Teddy. "Kathleen and I will wait out here while you go inside and ask for the wizard's eye."

Suddenly a terrible howl pierced the silence.

"Yikes!" said Annie.

"The wolves!" said Kathleen.

Teddy hurried to the door and threw it open. "Everyone inside!" he said.

And all four of them scrambled into the House of the Norns.

CHAPTER FIVE

The Norns

Teddy slammed the door against the wolves. Jack caught his breath.

"Welcome!" the three Norns said in unison. They all looked exactly alike, except they wore gowns of different colors—blue, brown, and gray.

"How are you, Jack, Annie, Teddy, and Kathleen?" said the blue Norn.

"We're good *now*," said Annie.

Jack was amazed that the Norns knew all their names. Despite their strange appearance, their friendly smiles and twinkling eyes put him at ease. In their cozy house, he began to feel warm for the first time since they had left home.

"Was your journey pleasant?" asked the brown Norn.

"Yes. We came in the Ice Wizard's sleigh," said Annie.

"With the help of a wind-string," said Teddy. Jack held up the string to show them.

The gray Norn cackled. "Yes, we know! I like a string with knots," she said.

"A string without knots would be a boring string indeed!" said the blue Norn.

"A *life* without knots would be a boring life indeed!" chimed in the brown Norn.

As they spoke, the Norns kept weaving. Their bulging eyes never blinked. Jack sensed that they never closed their eyes—or stopped their work.

"Sorry to bother you," said Annie. "But Jack and I need the eye of the Ice Wizard of Winter so we can save our friends Merlin and Morgan."

"We know," said the blue Norn. "We are weaving the story of the Ice Wizard now. Come look."

Jack moved with the others to the loom. Dozens of tiny pictures were woven into the tapestry. The threads were all wintry colors—blues, grays, and browns.

"The pictures tell the story of the wizard's life," explained the brown Norn.

One picture showed two children playing together. Another showed a boy running after a swan. Another showed two white wolves—and another showed an eye in a circle.

"What's the story of the eye?" Jack asked.

"Long ago, the Ice Wizard came to us seeking all the wisdom of the world," said the gray Norn. "We said we would give him wisdom if he gave us one of his eyes. He agreed to the bargain."

"The wizard doesn't seem very wise," said Annie.

"Indeed he is not," said the brown Norn. "We planted the seeds of wisdom in his heart, but they never grew."

"Why did you want his eye?" asked Jack.

"We wished to give it to the Frost Giant," said the blue Norn.

"*The Frost Giant?*" said Teddy. "Who is the Frost Giant?"

"He is neither magician nor mortal," said the blue Norn. "He is a blind force of nature that spares nothing in his path."

"We hoped the Frost Giant would use the wizard's eye to *see* the beauty of the world, so he might choose to *care* for it rather than destroy it," said the brown Norn. "But alas, the Frost Giant does not use our gift at all! Instead, he keeps it hidden away—right where we left it!"

"Where's that?" asked Annie.

"The Frost Giant sleeps inside the Hollow Hill," said the gray Norn.

"In the Hollow Hill is a hole," said the blue Norn.

"In the hole is a hailstone," said the brown Norn.

"And in the heart of the hailstone hides the wizard's eye," said the gray Norn.

Jack closed his eyes and repeated:

In the Hollow Hill is a hole.

In the hole is a hailstone.

In the heart of the hailstone
Hides the wizard's eye.

"Yes!" said the gray Norn. "That is where you must go. But beware: *You must never look directly at the Frost Giant. Anyone who looks directly at the Frost Giant will freeze to death at once.*"

Jack shivered and nodded.

"Well, we'd better get going," said Annie. "Thanks for your help. The Ice Wizard's rhyme tells us to pay you whatever you ask us to pay."

The Norns looked at each other. "I like that weaving around her neck," the gray Norn said to her sisters. "'Tis red like the fiery dawn." The other two Norns nodded eagerly.

"My scarf?" said Annie. "Sure. Here." She took off her red woolen scarf and placed it on the floor near the Norns' loom.

"Lovely!" said the blue Norn. "Perhaps we will stop weaving fates and start weaving scarves!"

The other Norns cackled. "Well, go now," said the gray Norn. "Travel toward the North Star. When you reach the snowy hills, look for the one whose peak is missing."

Jack, Annie, and Teddy started toward the door, but Kathleen stayed behind. "Forgive me, but I have one more question," she said. She pointed to the picture of the swan and the boy on the tapestry. "What is this story?"

"'Tis a sad tale," said the gray Norn. "The Ice Wizard had a younger sister who loved him more than anything in the world. One day they fought over something foolish. He lost his temper and told her to leave him alone forever. She ran down to the sea in tears. There she found a flock of swan maidens. They gave her a white feathered dress. She put on the dress and became a swan maiden herself. She flew away with the others and never returned."

"After that the Ice Wizard was never the same," said the blue Norn. "When his sister left, he grew cold and mean-spirited. 'Twas as if his sister took his heart with her when she flew away."

"That *is* sad," said Annie. "How will the Ice Wizard's story end?"

"You—not we—will determine the threads we weave next," said the brown Norn.

"We will?" said Annie.

"Yes," said the gray Norn. "Our powers are fading. Our plans no longer work the way we expect them to. The Ice Wizard has no wisdom! The Frost Giant has no sight! *You* must go now and finish the story."

The three sisters smiled at their visitors. Their skinny fingers fluttered over their weaving like butterflies over flowers.

Jack couldn't help smiling back at them. But then he thought about Merlin and Morgan. He thought about all the dangers waiting outside. "One last question," he said. "What's the story of the two white wolves?"

"Oh, the wolves!" said the blue Norn. "Do

not fear the wolves! A life without wolves would be a boring life indeed!" Her two sisters smiled in agreement. For the moment, their smiles made Jack feel unafraid of the white wolves— and the Ice Wizard and the Frost Giant, too.

"Good-bye! Good-bye! Good-bye!" said the three sisters.

Jack and the others waved good-bye. Then they slipped out of the House of the Norns and into the icy night.

CHAPTER SIX

In the Hollow Hill

Standing in the cold, Jack felt afraid again. There were big paw prints in the moonlit snow all around the house.

"The wolves were here," said Kathleen.

"Perhaps we should go back inside," said Teddy.

"No," said Kathleen. "We must walk with Jack and Annie back to the sleigh and send them on their journey to the Hollow Hill."

"Yes, of course," said Teddy, nodding.

As they all headed cautiously toward the

rocks, Jack glanced back at the House of the Norns. He wished they could return to its cozy warmth.

Kathleen put her hand on his shoulder. "Come," she said. "You must hurry."

Jack trudged with the others through the passage in the rocks. When they got to the other side, there was no sign of the two white wolves. The silver sleigh was waiting in the moonlight. Jack and Annie climbed inside it.

"Can't you come with us?" Jack asked Teddy and Kathleen. "Remember you said if we all work together, we can do anything?"

"Aye," said Teddy. "But what the Ice Wizard said is true. Only mortals can undo a bargain with the Fates."

"Do not fear," said Kathleen. "We will be with you in spirit. And we will meet you back at the wizard's palace at dawn."

"How will you get there?" asked Annie.

"I have a few rhymes I can try," said Teddy, smiling.

"And I have a bit of selkie magic," said Kathleen.

"And we have our wind-string!" said Annie.

"Hasten, then, to the Hollow Hill," said Kathleen.

"And remember what the Norns told you," said Teddy. "*Never* look at the Frost Giant."

"I know," said Jack. He pulled out the wind-string. He took off his gloves and untied a knot. A breeze began to blow.

Jack untied a second knot. The breeze grew stronger, the sail unfurled, and the runners slid forward.

Jack untied a third knot. The wind blew hard. The white sail snapped, and the sleigh took off through the night.

"Stand fast!" Teddy called after them.

Jack and Annie waved good-bye to Teddy and Kathleen as the sleigh slid swiftly over the sea ice. Soon the sleigh bumped onto the snow-covered plain and veered off sharply to the right.

"No, toward the North Star!" Jack called to Annie.

Annie turned the rudder, steering the sleigh back on course. They sailed toward the bright star in the distance.

As the silver runners swished across the windswept snow, Jack braced himself against the cold. He kept a lookout for the white wolves, but he didn't see any sign of them as the sleigh sped across the moonlit plain.

Soon he could see a row of snow-covered hills in the distance. "Look!" he said. "There it is!" He pointed to one of the hills—the only one without a peak.

"Tie her down!" Annie shouted.

Jack tied a knot in the string, and the sleigh began to slow down. He tied a second, then a third. The wind died down completely, and the sleigh coasted to a stop at the foot of the Hollow Hill. Jack and Annie climbed out.

Jack looked up at the steep white slope. "How do we get inside?" he said.

"I don't know," said Annie. "How do you think the Frost Giant gets inside?"

"Oh . . . the Frost Giant," said Jack. He really wished Teddy and Kathleen were with them. He felt as if part of their team was missing.

Annie seemed to read his thoughts. "We can do it," she said. "We have to—for Morgan and Merlin."

Jack nodded. "You're right," he said. They studied the hill in the moonlight.

"Up there—is that an opening?" said Annie.

"Maybe," said Jack. "Let's climb up and check it out." When they climbed a little way up the hill, Jack could clearly see a break in the snow-covered slope.

"Let's see if it leads inside!" said Annie.

"Wait, what about the Frost Giant?" said Jack.

"I have a feeling he's not here right now," said Annie. "We'd better go in and find the wizard's eye before he comes back."

"Okay," said Jack. "But be careful!"

They scurried farther up the slope. When they came to the opening, they stepped through the huge crack into the hill.

Jack and Annie found themselves on a ledge above a deep, rounded hollow. Moonlight flooded down through the open hilltop. At the bottom of the hollow was a flat spot where it looked as if the snow had been blown in circles.

"That must be where the giant sleeps!" said Annie.

"Yeah, and it's probably where he hides the eye," said Jack. "We just have to find a hole. Remember?" He repeated what the Norns had said:

In the Hollow Hill is a hole.
In the hole is a hailstone.
In the heart of the hailstone
Hides the wizard's eye.

"Right," said Annie.

Jack looked down at the snowy swirl. He looked back at Annie. "Onward?"

"Onward," she whispered.

Jack and Annie scrambled down into the hollow. Stepping carefully through the silver moonlight, they studied the ground, looking for the hole.

Annie stumbled and fell. "Whoa!" she said. "I think I just found the hole! I stepped in it!"

"Really?" said Jack. He knelt down beside her.

Annie reached down into a small hole in the floor of the hollow. "There's something in here!"

she said. She pulled out a chunk of ice the size of an egg. "The hailstone!"

In the dim light, it was impossible to see if anything was inside the ice chunk. "We don't know if this is the right hailstone," said Jack. "We'll have to wait till daylight to see if the eye's in there."

"It has to be the right one," said Annie. "How many hailstones are hidden in a hole in a hollow hill?"

"Good point," said Jack.

Annie turned the hailstone over in her hand. "Maybe the eye is looking at us now," she said.

"That's scientifically impossible," said Jack. "An eye can't see unless it's connected to a brain."

"Yeah, and a string can't make the wind blow, either," said Annie. "Forget science in this place. Wait—" She caught her breath. "Did you feel that?"

"Feel what?" said Jack.

"The ground's shaking," said Annie.

Jack *did* feel the ground trembling. He heard

a strange sound, too—a loud huffing sound coming from outside the hill—*HUFFFF, HUFFFF, HUFFFF. . . .* It sounded like breathing!

"The giant's back!" said Annie.

"Oh, no!" cried Jack.

The ground kept rumbling. The breathing sounds got louder.

"Hide the hailstone!" said Jack.

Annie shoved the ice chunk into her pocket.

HUFFFF, HUFFFF, HUFFFF. . . . It sounded like the giant was entering the hollow!

"He's coming!" said Annie.

"Hide!" whispered Jack.

Jack pulled Annie into the shadows. He remembered the gray Norn's warning: *Anyone who looks directly at the Frost Giant will freeze to death at once.*

"Whatever you do, *don't look at him!*" he whispered to Annie.

Crouching in the dark, they buried their faces in their hands and waited. . . .

CHAPTER SEVEN

The Frost Giant

*H*UFFFF, *HUFFFF, HUFFFFF.* . . . With each breath from the Frost Giant, a blast of cold wind swept through the hollow.

Jack trembled. He felt chilled to the bone. *HUFFFF, HUFFFF, HUFFFFF.* . . .

The giant's breathing grew louder and stronger. Jack squeezed his eyes shut as icy, wet wind rushed against his body.

HUFFFF, HUFFFF, HUFFFFF. . . .

Jack crouched lower and held on tightly to Annie.

HUFFFF, HUFFFF, HUFFFFF....

The giant's breath howled like a hundred ghosts through the hollow. Jack thought of the blue Norn's words: *He is a blind force of nature that spares nothing in his path....*

But then the giant's breathing seemed to grow a bit softer. *What's happening?* Jack wondered.

The breathing grew softer and softer. "Maybe he's going to sleep," Annie whispered.

The breathing became calm and steady. The wind died to a light breeze.

"I think the Frost Giant is sleeping," Annie whispered. "We should try to sneak out of here."

"Okay, but keep your eyes down. Just look at the ground!" whispered Jack.

"Right," whispered Annie.

Their heads bowed, Jack and Annie crept cautiously across the floor of the hollow and began climbing up toward the crack. Jack's teeth chattered, but he couldn't tell if it was from cold or fear.

Suddenly a deafening roar shook the night! The Frost Giant screamed with windy rage! He was awake!

Jack was blown to the ground. He tried to crawl across the snow, but he didn't know which way to go, and he was afraid to look up.

"Jack! This way!" Annie's voice called above the roar of the giant's breath. She helped him up and they struggled together against the wind. Finally they came to the crack in the wall.

Jack and Annie scrambled through the crack. Outside, the wild wind knocked them over, and they tumbled down the side of the hill.

The wind swirled the snow across the plain. "Annie! Annie!" Jack called. Where was she? Where was the sleigh? He couldn't see anything. He couldn't stay on his feet.

The wind roared even louder. An avalanche of snow came crashing down the hillside. When it hit the ground, the snow exploded into great clouds of white powder.

"Jack! Jack!"

Jack heard Annie's voice in the screaming wind. He tried to stand up. But snow kept falling on top of him, until he was completely covered.

As Jack lay buried under the snow, all his strength left his body. He knew he should dig his way out, but he was too cold and too tired. He was too tired to look for Annie. He was too tired to fight the Frost Giant. Instead, he closed his eyes and drifted into an icy sleep.

❋ ❋ ❋

Jack dreamed that cold fur was brushing against his face. He dreamed that a wolf was digging around him, nudging him, pushing him, sniffing him. . . .

Jack opened his eyes. He felt dazed. At first he couldn't see. But he could feel that he wasn't buried in snow anymore. He wiped off his glasses. He saw a low moon and some stars in a clear sky.

The Frost Giant must have left, Jack thought. But then he heard a panting noise. He sat up and looked around. One of the white wolves was crouching right behind him!

Jack scrambled to his feet. "Go away!" he shouted.

The wolf stepped back and growled.

"Go! Go! Go!" shouted Jack. He picked up handfuls of snow and threw them at the wolf.

The wolf backed away a few more feet. Jack looked around wildly. Annie was lying very still on top of the snow. The other white wolf was sniffing and pawing at her.

Jack's anger made him fearless. "Leave her alone!" he shouted. "Go away!" He scooped up more snow and threw it.

The wolf stepped back.

"GO! GO!" shouted Jack. "Get away! Leave us alone!" He glared angrily at the two white wolves.

The wolves stared back at Jack. Their yellow eyes gleamed.

"I'm not kidding—GO!" shouted Jack.

Jack stared fiercely at the wolves. Finally the wolves looked away. They glanced at each other and then slowly backed off. They looked at Jack and Annie one last time. Then they turned and trotted away over the snow.

Jack rushed to Annie. He knelt beside her and lifted her head. "Wake up! Wake up!" he said.

Annie opened her eyes.

"You okay?" Jack asked.

"Yes . . . I dreamed about white wolves," Annie murmured.

"Me too!" said Jack. "And then when I woke up, they were here! They were about to eat us!"

"Really?" Annie sat up and looked around.

"Yeah, but I scared them off," said Jack.

"What about the Frost Giant?" Annie said.

"He's gone, too," said Jack. "Come on. Let's get out of here!" Jack helped Annie up from the snow. "Do you still have the wizard's eye?"

Annie felt in her pocket. "Got it," she said.

"Good." Jack looked around. Beyond the

heaps of fallen snow, the silver sleigh was waiting for them. Overhead, the sky had turned to a light shade of gray.

"It's almost dawn," said Jack. "Remember what the wizard said? We have to bring back his eye by the break of day—or we'll never see Merlin or Morgan again!"

Jack held Annie's hand and they trudged together through the snow. When they got to the sleigh, they climbed inside. Annie took her place at the rudder. Jack pulled out the wind-string and untied a knot.

The breeze rocked the sleigh. Jack untied a second knot, and the sail began to fill. He untied a third, and the silver sleigh moved forward, gliding over the white ground.

Swish—swish—swish. The sleigh moved through the thick snow and away from the Hollow Hill. As they sailed over the white plain, the sky was turning from gray to pale pink.

"We have to go faster!" said Annie.

Jack untied a fourth knot. The wind whistled in his ears. The sleigh picked up speed. Annie steered it past the rocks and over the sea ice. She steered it over the plain, south to the palace of the Ice Wizard.

When the sleigh drew close to the palace, Jack tied a knot, and they began to slow down. He tied three more, and the sleigh came to a stop.

Jack and Annie looked around in the faint, cold light. "I wonder where Teddy and Kathleen are," said Annie. "They said they'd meet us here at dawn."

Jack studied the vast white plain, but he saw no sign of their friends. He wished he had Kathleen's vision. "I hope they're okay," he said. "I hope they didn't run into the white wolves."

"I have a feeling the wolves wouldn't hurt them," said Annie. "The wolf in my dream seemed nice."

"Dream wolves are different from real wolves," said Jack.

"I don't think we can wait for them," said

Annie. "The eye has to be back by the time the sun comes up."

"The eye!" said Jack. "We never looked to see if it was inside the hailstone."

Annie reached in her pocket and pulled out the hailstone. She held it up.

Jack gasped. Staring out at him from inside the ice was an eyeball. It was about the size of a large marble. The eyeball was white with a sparkling blue center.

"Oh, man," whispered Jack.

"It's beautiful, isn't it?" said Annie.

"I don't know about that." Jack felt a little queasy. Seeing an eye outside of a human head was too weird for him. "Put it away for now," he said.

Annie put the hailstone back in her pocket. Jack looked around again. The sky had brightened from pale pink to red. A thin sliver of the sun was peeking over the horizon.

"The sun!" cried Jack. "Hurry!" He and Annie jumped out of the sleigh and charged toward the palace.

When they got to the entrance, Annie stopped. "Look!" she said, pointing to big paw prints in the snow. "Wolf tracks!"

"Oh, no," said Jack. "Do you think the white wolves are inside? That's weird."

"It doesn't matter! We have to go in! Hurry!" said Annie. They rushed into the palace—just as the fiery ball of the sun rose over the horizon.

CHAPTER EIGHT

Return of the Eye

Jack and Annie walked through the front hall of the palace, past the ice columns, and into the wizard's throne room. The walls and floor glittered with the brilliant, cold light of dawn.

"Uh-oh," said Jack.

The wizard was waiting for them—and the two white wolves were sleeping on either side of his throne. Jack was confused. *Why are they here?* he wondered. *Do they belong to the wizard?*

The wolves lifted their heads and sniffed the air. Their ears pricked up. When they caught sight of Jack and Annie, they sprang to their feet. They stared at them with piercing yellow eyes.

The Ice Wizard was staring intently at Jack and Annie, too. "Well?" he said. "Did you bring back my eye?"

"Yes," said Jack.

Annie took the hailstone out of her pocket and held it up to the wizard. Jack watched the wolves nervously as the hailstone passed from Annie's small hand into the wizard's large, rough hand.

The wizard stared down at the chunk of ice. Then he looked at Jack and Annie. "Indeed, you *are* heroes," he said breathlessly.

"Not really," Jack murmured.

The wizard looked again at his eye inside the hailstone. Then, with a quick movement, he slammed the ice chunk against the arm of his throne.

Jack and Annie gasped and stepped back. The wizard slammed the hailstone against his throne again. This time, the ice cracked.

The wizard gently pried his eye out of the

heart of the hailstone. He lifted the frozen eye-ball into the air and studied it in the light. Then, with an eager cry, he ripped off his eye patch.

Jack and Annie watched in amazement as the wizard fitted the eye into its dark, empty socket. Jack held his breath. He was horrified, yet fascinated. He couldn't imagine someone just shoving an eye back into his head.

The wizard slowly lowered his hand. He seemed to be holding his breath. He had two eyes. But the new one didn't move. It looked as if it was still frozen.

Jack grew worried. If the eye didn't work, the wizard might not help them. "We—we brought you your eye," he said. "So can you tell us where Merlin and Morgan are now?"

The wizard jerked his head to look at Jack. He covered one eye with his hand. Then he covered the other. In a frenzy, he went back and forth, covering and uncovering each eye.

Finally the wizard dropped his hand and

roared, "NO!" The wizard's howl shook the ice
columns. "You have tricked me!"

"No we haven't," said Annie.

"This eye is useless!" cried the wizard. "It
has no life! No sight!"

"But that's the eye you gave to the Norns,"

said Annie. "You promised if we brought it back, you'd give us Merlin and Morgan."

The two white wolves threw back their heads and howled.

"NO!" cried the wizard. "You tricked me! You tricked me!"

"Let's get out of here," whispered Jack. He pulled Annie toward the ice columns.

"STOP!" shouted the wizard. "YOU CAN-NOT ESCAPE ME!" He grabbed Merlin's Staff of Strength. The wolves growled and yelped. The wizard pointed the staff at Jack and Annie. He started to say a spell—"RO-EEE—"

"WAIT!" someone yelled. Teddy burst into the throne room. "Wait! Wait!"

The wizard held his staff in the air. He stared wildly at Teddy. His face was twisted with rage.

"We have something for you!" Teddy shouted at the wizard. "Kathleen!" he called.

Kathleen stepped out from behind the ice columns. With her was a young woman with long braids. The woman wore a flowing dress. Around her shoulders was a white feathered cloak. Her eyes rested on the wizard, and a radiant smile spread over her face. She began walking slowly toward the throne.

The wizard lowered Merlin's Staff of Strength. He stared back at the young woman. All the color drained from his face. For a long moment, he was as still as a statue. Then an ice-blue tear leaked out of his frozen eye and ran down his white cheek.

Jack and Annie stood with Kathleen and

Teddy. They all watched the young woman and the Ice Wizard gaze silently at each other.

"Is she his sister, the swan maiden?" whispered Annie.

"Yes," whispered Kathleen.

The swan maiden spoke to the Ice Wizard in a strange language—*"Val-ee-ven-o-wan."*

The wizard did not answer. Tears flowed gently now from both his eyes.

"Val-ee-ven-o-wan," the swan maiden said again.

"What's she saying?" Jack asked.

"She is saying, *I have come back to forgive you,*" said Kathleen.

The wizard stood up. He walked down the steps from his throne. He gently touched the swan maiden's face, as if to make sure she was real. Then he answered her softly in the strange language. "*Fel-o-wan.*"

"How did you find her?" Jack asked Teddy.

"A seal took us under the ice to the Isle of the Swans," said Teddy.

"When we found her, I told her how much the wizard has missed her," said Kathleen. "I also told her about the two of you and how you always help each other. I told her she should return to her brother and be his friend again."

The wizard and his sister kept speaking softly to each other in their strange language. Warm sunlight shimmered through the palace windows.

Annie stepped forward. "Um—excuse me," she said.

The wizard looked at her. "My sister has returned home," he said with wonder. "I can see with both eyes now. I can see perfectly."

"I'm glad," said Annie. "But now you must give Merlin and Morgan back to us."

The wizard looked at his sister. She nodded. The wizard held out Merlin's Staff of Strength. "Use this to bring them back," he said. "Hold it tightly and call out for them." He gave the staff to Annie.

Annie could barely lift it by herself. "Hold it with me, Jack," she said.

Jack stepped forward and grabbed the magic staff. The smooth, golden wood felt warm and vibrant in his hands.

As they gripped the staff together, Annie threw back her head and called out: "Merlin and Morgan, come back!"

A long burst of blue light shot out of the end of the staff—and flashed toward the two white wolves.

Suddenly wolf eyes changed into human eyes! Wolf noses changed into human noses! Wolf mouths changed into human mouths! Wolf ears into human ears! Wolf paws into human hands and feet! Wolf fur into long red cloaks!

The two white wolves were gone, and a man and a woman stood in their places.

CHAPTER NINE

Wisdom of the Heart

"Merlin! Morgan!" shouted Annie.

Teddy and Kathleen cried out in amazement.

Annie rushed to Morgan and hugged her.

Jack was filled with giddy relief. "Hi!" he said. "Hi!"

"Welcome back, sir!" Teddy said to Merlin.

"Thank you," said Merlin. He looked at Jack and Annie. "And thank you for turning us back into ourselves."

"We didn't know you and Morgan were the wolves!" Annie said.

"We were following you so we could help you," said Morgan.

"The wizard told us that if you caught up with us, you would eat us!" said Jack.

"Really?" said Morgan.

They all looked at the Ice Wizard. Standing with his sister, he stared guiltily at Morgan and Merlin.

"I feared that if they got close to you, they might discover who you were," he said. "But I will do no more harm, I promise—for I can see clearly now." The wizard looked back at his sister, and his blue eyes shined with joy.

"You can see because you have your heart back," said Morgan. "It was not only your eye that was missing—it was also your heart. We see with our hearts as well as our eyes."

"And now perhaps you can find the wisdom you were seeking from the Norns," said Merlin, "for wisdom is knowledge learned with the heart as well as the head."

The Ice Wizard nodded. "Please find it in *your* hearts to forgive me," he said. "Use my sleigh to take you safely home."

"Yes, indeed, we must leave now," said Morgan. "We have been gone from Camelot too long."

"The next time you come to Camelot, my friend, you must come as a guest," said Merlin, "not as a thief in the night."

"And you must bring your sister also," Morgan said to the wizard.

"Indeed I will," the wizard said.

Merlin looked at Jack, Annie, Teddy, and Kathleen. "Is everyone ready to leave now?" he asked.

"Yes, sir," they all answered together.

Merlin looked at the Staff of Strength in Jack's hands.

"Oh! Sorry, I almost forgot," said Jack. He handed the heavy staff to Merlin.

As soon as Merlin held the Staff of Strength, he seemed more powerful. "Let us be off!" he said briskly.

Merlin and Morgan led the way out of the throne room, their red cloaks billowing behind them. Teddy and Kathleen followed, and Jack and Annie hurried after them.

Just before they left the room, Jack and Annie glanced back at the Ice Wizard and his swan sister. They were deep in conversation again.

"They haven't seen each other for years," said Annie. "They must have a lot to talk about."

"Yeah," said Jack. He couldn't imagine not seeing Annie for years. "Come on, let's go." He took her hand and pulled her out of the throne room, through the front hall, and into the cold dawn.

Jack and Annie followed their four Camelot friends to the wizard's sleigh. Everyone climbed in.

Annie sat at the rudder. Jack stood at the front. He pulled out the wind-string and untied a knot. The sleigh rocked forward. He untied another, and the sleigh started moving very slowly.

The sleigh was heavier than before, so Jack quickly untied two more knots. The sleigh bolted across the snow.

"Stand fast!" said Teddy.

As the sleigh swished through the dawn, Annie turned to Morgan and Merlin. "I have a question," she said. "Can you tell us what the giant looks like—the Frost Giant?"

Merlin smiled. "There is no Frost Giant," he said.

"*What?*" said Kathleen and Teddy.

"Sure there is," said Annie. "We heard his breathing!"

"He nearly froze us to death!" said Jack.

"At night, the wind often swirls through the Hollow Hill like a cyclone," said Merlin. "You experienced one of those storms."

"But what about the Norns' story of giving the wizard's eye to the Frost Giant as a gift?" said Jack.

"Many ancient peoples believe that the forces

of nature are actual giants or monsters," said Morgan. "The Norns are the last of their kind. They hold to the idea that the Frost Giant is a living creature who haunts the Hollow Hill. In truth, the Frost Giant never accepted their gift because there is no Frost Giant."

Jack shook his head. "We believed what the Norns believed. They told us we'd freeze to death if we looked directly at the Frost Giant."

"And we believed what the wizard told us, too," said Annie, "that the wolves would eat us if they caught up to us!"

"People often try to convince us that the world is scarier than it truly is," said Morgan.

Right now the world didn't seem at all scary to Jack. Everything was calm and bright. Soft, rose-colored light was breaking through the morning clouds.

"Today is the first day after the winter solstice," said Morgan. "Today the light starts to return. The days will grow longer."

Jack turned to look at the sun. He caught sight of the tree house sitting on top of a snowdrift, not far away.

Jack tied a knot in the wind-string. He tied three more, and the sleigh came to a stop at the foot of the snowdrift.

Merlin looked at them. "On the winter solstice, you showed great courage," he said. "You endured storms and terror and extraordinary cold. You reunited the Ice Wizard and the swan maiden. And perhaps most important, you retrieved my Staff of Strength. I thank you."

"Sure," Jack and Annie said modestly.

"You have done much for the kingdom of Camelot on your last four missions," said Merlin. "On your next adventure, you will have a mission back in your world—in real time, not in the time of myth and magicians."

"We will call for you again soon," said Morgan.

"Great!" said Annie.

Jack and Annie climbed out of the sleigh. They looked back at Teddy and Kathleen. "I hope you will help us with our next journey, too," said Annie.

Teddy smiled. "If we all work together, we can do anything, aye?" he said.

"Aye!" said Jack and Annie together. Then they turned and trudged up the snowdrift. At the top, they climbed into the window of the tree house. Once they were inside, they looked back.

The sleigh was gone.

"Bye," Annie said softly.

Jack picked up the small gray stone from the floor. He pointed at the words *Frog Creek* in the wizard's message. "I wish we could go there," he said.

The wind started to blow.

It blew harder and harder.

Then everything was still.

Absolutely still.

❄ ❄ ❄

Jack opened his eyes. They were back in the Frog Creek woods. No time at all had passed while they'd been gone. It was almost twilight. Snowflakes fell like tiny feathers outside the tree house window.

Annie shivered. "I'm cold," she said.

"Here—take my scarf," said Jack. He pulled off his scarf.

"No, you need it," said Annie.

"No, take it. I'll be okay." Jack put his scarf around Annie's neck. "What will you tell Mom when she asks about *your* scarf?" he asked.

"I'll just tell her the Sisters of Fate took it as payment for telling us how to find the eye of the Ice Wizard in a hole in the Hollow Hill," said Annie.

"Right," said Jack, laughing.

"We'd better get home before dark," said Annie. She started down the rope ladder. Jack followed her.

As they stepped onto the ground, Jack remembered the wind-string. "We forgot to give this back," he said. He reached into his pocket and pulled out the string. "I guess Merlin's magic took the sleigh back to Camelot."

Jack and Annie looked at the string for a moment. "Untie a knot," Annie whispered.

Jack took off his gloves and untied a knot. He held his breath and waited. Nothing happened. He gave Annie a little smile. "I guess in our world, it's just a piece of string," he said.

Jack put the string back in his pocket. He and Annie started walking over the snowy ground between the trees. As they walked, Jack looked for Teddy's and Kathleen's footprints. But they were completely gone.

Jack and Annie moved out of the woods and down their street. They saw Christmas tree lights sparkling in people's houses and candles shining in windows.

Their boots squeaked as they crossed their snow-covered yard. When they got to the stairs of the porch, Jack stopped. He stared in astonishment.

Annie's red woolen scarf was draped over the railing of the porch.

"I don't believe it!" said Jack.

"I do!" said Annie.

They hurried up the stairs and Annie grabbed her scarf. "Look!" she said.

She held up the scarf to show Jack. There

was a tiny picture woven into it: a picture of him and Annie and two white wolves.

Jack was speechless.

"Cool, huh?" said Annie. She gave Jack back his scarf. Then she tied her scarf around her neck. She tucked the part with the picture under her jacket collar.

The front door opened. A delicious smell wafted out from the house.

"Hi!" said their mom. "The cookies are ready. Come inside and get warm!"

A Note from the Author

Some time ago I wrote a book called *Favorite Norse Myths*. In that book, I retold the myths of the Viking people, who lived long ago in the icy, rugged lands of Scandinavia. While I was working on *Winter of the Ice Wizard*, several elements from the Norse myths inspired the plot of my story. For instance, the Norse myths tell about a god named Odin who traded his eye for all the wisdom of the world, and they tell about Frost Giants, who represent the most brutal forces of nature. There are also three sister goddesses known as the Norns who decide the future. (In Greek mythology, three sisters called the Fates determine the future.)

While doing further research on the old legends of Nordic lands, I came across the swan maidens, women who could turn into swans, as well as wind-ropes (or wind-strings). I found out that wizards sold ropes with knots of wind to seafarers to help their ships sail across the ocean. Wind-strings are also mentioned in Hans Christian Andersen's story "The Snow Queen." The reindeer in "The Snow Queen" says that he can "twist all the winds of the world together in a knot. If a seaman loosens one knot, then he has a good wind."

Winter of the Ice Wizard closes this quartet of Merlin Missions. On these four missions, Jack and Annie find magical treasures for Merlin: water from the Cauldron of Memory and Imagination, the Diamond of Destiny, the Sword of Light, and the Staff of Strength. These four things were inspired by the Four Hallows of Camelot, which, according to Irish legend, were the four most sacred gifts of the ancient Celtic people.

Fun Activities for Jack and Annie and *You*!

Wizard Eye

Jack and Annie had to travel to the Frost Giant's home to find the Ice Wizard's eye, but you can make your own!

You will need:

- Two Popsicle sticks or tongue depressors
- Glue (optional)
- Multicolored yarn or yarn in your favorite colors
- Scissors

1. Start your wizard eye by holding the two sticks at a 90-degree angle—one stick should be vertical and the other should be horizontal, making a plus sign. Or, for added stability, you can hold one stick vertically and put a dab of glue in the middle. Then glue the other stick horizontally, and let dry overnight.

2. Loop the yarn once around one of the four sticks, close to the center. Then knot the yarn so that it stays in place.

3. Loop the yarn across the center of the crossed sticks in the same direction twice, and then switch directions and wrap it twice in the other direction. This will make an X with yarn over the center of your wizard eye.

4. Hold the yarn between two sticks and bring it under and around the stick to the left. Make sure it is pulled as close to the center of your wizard eye as possible.

5. Bring the yarn under and around the next stick to the left.

6. Keep moving counterclockwise around the sticks. As you loop the yarn under, make sure that it lies next to but never on top of the yarn that was previously looped.

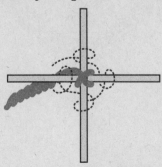

7. If you are using different-colored yarn, you can cut the end of one of the colors of yarn and tie it to a new color. Then continue moving

counterclockwise until you want to change colors again.

8. When you are about half an inch from the ends of the sticks, knot the yarn on the stick that you want to be the top.

9. Cut the yarn, leaving about an eight-inch tail so that you can hang your wizard eye on a wall, in a window, or anywhere you like!

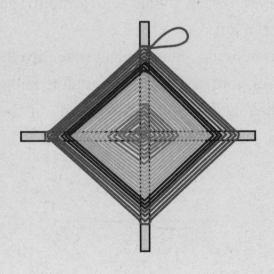

Puzzle of the Ice Wizard

Jack and Annie learned some important lessons in the Land-Behind-the-Clouds. Answer the following questions to put your knowledge of *Winter of the Ice Wizard* to the test.

You can use a notebook or make a copy of this page if you don't want to write in your book.

1. The shortest day of the year is called the winter _ _ _ _ _ _ _.

☐ ☐ ☐ ☐ ☐ ☐ ◯ ☐

2. The Ice Wizard's sister was a _ _ _ _ maiden.

☐ ☐ ☐ ◯

3. Jack and Annie are warned never to look at the _ _ _ _ _ Giant.

☐ ◯ ☐ ☐ ☐

4. Who are also known as the Sisters of Fate?

☐ ◯ ☐ ☐ ☐

5. The Sisters of Fate wear brown, gray, and what color?

☐ ☐ ○ ☐

6. The Ice Wizard's eye is hidden in this.

☐ ☐ ○ ☐ ☐ ☐ ☐ ☐ ☐

7. Merlin's staff is called the Staff of

_ _ _ _ _ _ _ _.

☐ ☐ ☐ ☐ ○ ☐ ☐ ☐

Now look at your answers above. The letters that are circled spell a word—but that word is scrambled! Can you unscramble the letters to complete the following sentence? The Sisters of Fate weave tapestries. A famous tapestry that you can visit at the Cloisters in New York City features this mythical creature:

a _ _ _ _ _ _ _.

Here's a special preview of

Magic Tree House® *#33*
(A Merlin Mission)
Carnival at Candlelight

Jack and Annie must go to Venice, Italy,
to save the Grand Lady of the Lagoon
from a terrible disaster!

Available now!

CHAPTER ONE

A Book of Magic

Dawn was breaking in the Frog Creek woods. Jack saw a light shining up ahead. He ran toward it. He ran so fast, he couldn't hear his feet hitting the ground. He couldn't feel the frosty winter air.

As Jack got closer to the light, he could see the magic tree house at the top of the tallest oak. A girl and boy were looking out the window. The girl had dark, wavy hair and sea-blue eyes. The boy had tousled red hair and a big grin on his face. As the two kids waved at him, Jack felt incredibly happy.

"Jack, wake up!"

Jack opened his eyes. His sister, Annie, was standing beside his bed. She was wearing her winter jacket. It was barely light outside.

"I just had a dream about the tree house," she said.

"Really?" Jack said sleepily.

"I dreamed we were running through the woods at dawn," said Annie, "and when we got to the tree house, Teddy and Kathleen were there waiting for us."

Jack sat up. "I just had the same dream!" he said.

"Meet you downstairs," said Annie.

Annie left Jack's room. Jack jumped out of bed, put on his glasses, and threw on his clothes. He grabbed his winter jacket and his backpack. Then he slipped quietly down the stairs and out the front door.

Annie was waiting on the porch. The February air was chilly. Frost sparkled in the grass as the sun rose over the Frog Creek woods.

"Ready?" asked Annie.

Jack nodded and zipped his jacket. Without another word, he and Annie hurried up their street and headed into the woods. They ran through the long shadows of early morning, between the bare winter trees. Then they stopped.

The tree house *was* back, just as Jack had seen it in his dream! It was high in the tallest oak tree, shining in the cold morning light.

"Wow," breathed Jack. "Dreams *can* come true."

"Yep," said Annie. "Teddy! Kathleen!"

No one answered.

"I guess only part of this dream came true," Annie said sadly. She grabbed the rope ladder and started up. Jack followed. Annie climbed into the tree house. "Oh, wow!" she said.

"What is it?" said Jack.

"They're here!" said Annie in a loud whisper.

Jack climbed in behind her. Their friends

Teddy and Kathleen, apprentices to Morgan le Fay, were sitting under the tree house window. Wrapped in heavy woolen cloaks, they were both fast asleep.

"Hey, sleepyheads!" said Annie. "Wake up!"

Kathleen blinked and yawned. Teddy rubbed his eyes. When he saw Jack and Annie, he gave them a wide grin and leapt to his feet. "Hello!" he said.

"Hello!" cried Annie. She threw her arms around Teddy. "We both dreamed you were here."

"Ah, then our magic worked!" said Teddy. "Kathleen suggested we send dreams to let you know we were here, and it seems our magic sent *us* to dreamland as well."

"But now we are all awake," said Kathleen. "And I am very glad to see you." She stood up, drawing her cloak around her. Her blue eyes sparkled like seawater in the dawn light.

"I'm glad to see you, too," Jack said shyly.

"Are you taking us on another Merlin Mission?" said Annie.

"Not exactly," said Teddy. "Merlin has a most important mission for you. But this time, we will not be going along."

"Oh, no!" said Annie. "What if we need your magic to help us?"

Teddy and Kathleen looked at each other and smiled. Then Kathleen turned back to Jack and Annie. "Morgan thinks you may be ready to use magic on your own," she said.

"Really?" said Jack.

"Yes," said Teddy, "but Merlin is *very* cautious about sharing magic powers with mortals, even with two as worthy as you. He is also wary of magic being used outside the realm of Camelot. Nevertheless, Morgan has convinced Merlin to let you prove yourselves. You will be tested on four missions."

"But we don't know any magic," said Jack.

"Remember what I told you on our last

adventure?" said Teddy. "If we all work together—"

"Anything is possible!" said Annie. "But you just said you weren't coming with us."

"That is true," said Kathleen. "And that is why we bring you *this*." She reached into a pocket of her cloak and pulled out a small hand-made book. She gave the book to Annie.

The cover of the book was made of rough brown paper. Written on it in neat, simple handwriting was the title:

10
Magic Rhymes
for
Annie and Jack
from
Teddy and Kathleen

"You made this for us?" said Annie.

"Yes," said Kathleen. "One line of each rhyme is in Teddy's language, and one is in mine, the language of the Seal People."

Annie opened the book to the table of contents. She and Jack skimmed the list of rhymes, and Jack read some of the entries aloud:

Fly Through the Air. Make Metal Soft. Turn into Ducks—"

Annie giggled. "These are so cool!" she said. "Let's all turn into ducks!"

"Not now," said Kathleen. "You must use these rhymes very sparingly. There are only ten rhymes in the book, and each can only be used once. They are meant to last you for four journeys."

"Four?" said Jack.

"Aye," said Teddy. "Merlin has agreed that if you can use our magic wisely on four missions, he will teach you the secrets that will allow you to make magic on your own."

"Oh, boy!" said Annie.

Jack put the book of magic rhymes in his backpack. "So where are we going on our first mission?" he asked.

"This research book from Morgan will tell you," said Teddy. He took out a book and handed it to Jack. The cover showed a bright, colorful city surrounded by water.

Jack read the title aloud:

A VISIT TO VENICE, ITALY.

"I've heard of Venice," said Annie. "Last year Aunt Gail and Uncle Michael went there on vacation."

"Aye, 'tis a city that has long welcomed travelers," said Teddy. "But you and Jack will travel to the Venice of two hundred sixty years ago."

"What will we do there?" asked Jack.

"Merlin has prepared careful directions for you," said Teddy. He pulled a letter out of a pocket in his cloak and gave it to Jack. "Read this when you get to Venice."

"Okay," said Jack. He put Merlin's letter and Morgan's research book into his backpack.

"Wait a minute," said Annie. "If we take the tree house to Venice, how will you guys get back to Camelot?"

Teddy and Kathleen smiled and held up their hands. They each wore a ring made of pale blue glass. "These magic rings belong to Morgan," said Kathleen. "They will take us home."

"Remember," Teddy said to Jack and Annie. "Follow Merlin's directions carefully. If you prove yourselves to be wise and brave helpers, he will call for you again soon."

Kathleen nodded. "Good-bye now," she said to Jack and Annie. "Good luck."

Kathleen and Teddy raised their glass rings to their lips. Together they whispered words too softly to be heard, then blew on the rings.

Before Jack and Annie's eyes, the two young sorcerers began to fade into the cool morning air. In an instant, they had disappeared completely.

"They're gone," breathed Jack.

"I guess it's time for us to go, too," said Annie.

Jack took a deep breath. Then he pointed at the cover of the Venice book. "I wish we could go there!" he said.

The wind started to blow.

The tree house started to spin.

It spun faster and faster.

Then everything was still.

Absolutely still.

Adventure awaits at
MagicTreeHouse.com

You've Read the Books . . . Now Play the Games!

Join Jack and Annie on brand-new missions and play the Fact Tracker Showdown!

Exclusive to You!
Use this code to unlock a bonus game!

REWARD CODE

WOLVES

MAGIC TREE HOUSE®

MTH32

RHCB

Love learning with Jack and Annie?
Then track the facts with your favorite
brother-and-sister team in these
Magic Tree House® Fact Trackers!

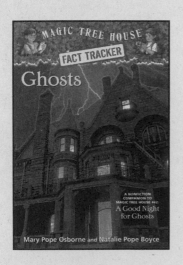

MAGIC TREE HOUSE

FACT TRACKER

Ghosts

A NONFICTION
COMPANION TO
MAGIC TREE HOUSE #42:
A Good Night
for Ghosts

Mary Pope Osborne and Natalie Pope Boyce

MAGIC TREE HOUSE

FACT TRACKER

Sabertooths and the
Ice Age

A NONFICTION
COMPANION TO
MAGIC TREE HOUSE #7:
Sunset of the
Sabertooth

Mary Pope Osborne and Natalie Pope Boyce

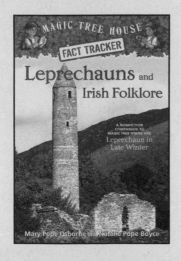

MAGIC TREE HOUSE

FACT TRACKER

Leprechauns and
Irish Folklore

A NONFICTION
COMPANION TO
MAGIC TREE HOUSE #43:
Leprechaun in
Late Winter

Mary Pope Osborne and Natalie Pope Boyce

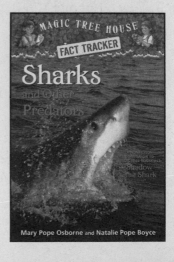

MAGIC TREE HOUSE

FACT TRACKER

Sharks
and Other
Predators

A NONFICTION
COMPANION TO
MAGIC TREE HOUSE #53:
Shadow
of the Shark

Mary Pope Osborne and Natalie Pope Boyce

Have you read all of the Magic Tree House® books?

Merlin Missions

Plus Magic Tree House® Fact Trackers
and more! For a full list of titles, visit
MagicTreeHouse.com

BRING MAGIC TREE HOUSE TO YOUR SCHOOL!

Magic Tree House musicals now available for performance by young people!

Ask your teacher or director
to contact
Music Theatre International
for more information:
BroadwayJr.com
Licensing@MTIshows.com
(212) 541-4684

ATTENTION, TEACHERS!

Classroom Adventures Program

The Magic Tree House **CLASSROOM ADVENTURES PROGRAM** is a free, comprehensive set of online educational resources for teachers developed by Mary Pope Osborne as a gift to teachers, to thank them for their enthusiastic support of the series. Educators can learn more at MTHClassroomAdventures.org.

MAGIC TREE HOUSE